Postman Pat™
annual 1991

£4.25

This book belongs to

name ....

address ....

.... postcode ....

Written by John Broadhead and Joyce McAleer
Illustrated by Edgar Hodges and Bill Mevin

Copyright © Woodland Animations Ltd, 1990

Published in Great Britain by World International
Publishing Limited, an Egmont Company,
Egmont House, PO Box 111,
Great Ducie Street, Manchester M60 3BL.

Printed in Italy   1st Reprint

ISBN 0 7235 6890 1

Contents

Welcome to Greendale

Meet the folk who live in the village of Greendale.
It doesn't happen very often, but today they have gathered together outside Greendale Church just for **you**!

You know Pat and Jess, of course, but do you know everyone else? Look at the bottom of the page and you'll find the answers.

1 Pat Clifton; 2 Sara Clifton; 3 Julian Clifton; 4 Jess; 5 Colonel Forbes; 6 Doctor Gilbertson; 7 Reverend Timms; 8 Mrs Goggins; 9 Granny Dryden; 10 Ted Glen; 11 Miss Hubbard; 12 Julia Pottage; 13 Tom Pottage; 14 Katy Pottage; 15 PC Selby; 16 Peter Fogg; 17 Alf Thompson; 18 Dorothy Thompson; 19 Sam Waldron; 20 George Lancaster.

Pat's birthday surprise

"See you later, Pat!"

It was Pat's birthday. What a pity that Sara and Julian were not yet awake to wish him many happy returns!

Miss Hubbard's bicycle was not outside her house. "Where can she be at this time of day?" wondered Pat, as he posted her letters.

Pat had a parcel for Granny Dryden but she wasn't at home to take it from him! "I'll bring it back tomorrow," he sighed.

"Ted is usually hard at work by now," said Pat, stroking his chin thoughtfully. "Is there **no one** I can tell about my birthday?"

Greendale Farm was empty too – except for the animals, of course! But cows aren't very interested in people's birthdays, are they?

"I've never seen the village so quiet," Pat told Jess, as they drove back towards the post office. "Even PC Selby is missing!"

But there was a lovely treat waiting for them! Mrs Goggins had planned a surprise party for Pat and **everyone** was there!

Granny Dryden's kitchen

Hello, readers! I'd like to show you two special Greendale cakes you can make with the help of a grown-up. They're tasty by themselves or you can make smaller ones to place on top of your birthday or Christmas cake. I hope you enjoy them!

Pat's van

Ask a grown-up to bake or buy a slab sponge cake. Cut it as shown in the picture, then cover it with dark pink icing. Add windows, headlights, handles and wheels by piping carefully with chocolate icing. Mmm!

Pat's post-box

Stand a piece of Swiss roll cake on its end on a plate and cover it with dark pink icing. Then add another layer of icing on the top only, making little dents round the edge. Finally draw the letter-slot, door and badge with chocolate piping. Delicious!

A night at the theatre

What's **this**? Has Postman Pat given up his job and become a bus driver? No, as usual he was just helping the people of Greendale!

He was taking a group of them to the big theatre in Pencaster to see the pantomime called **Robin Hood and his Merry Men**!

It was a very good show. Granny Dryden and Miss Hubbard laughed out loud at the funny tricks Robin played on the Sheriff of Nottingham.

Then the manager came on stage. "Will the driver of a minibus, number RKC 694T, please move it," he said. "It's blocking the traffic . . ."

11

"That's our bus," cried Pat, "but I thought I'd parked it carefully!" He stood up and made his way along the row to the exit.

"It's not in anyone's way," Pat murmured. But he didn't see the group of men in strange old clothes creeping up on him!

"Hey! What's going on?" he shouted, as the men put a blindfold on him. "Don't worry, we won't hurt you!" laughed one of them.

Back in the theatre, the pantomime had begun again. "Where can Pat be?" asked Tom Pottage. "Wait and see!" answered Sara with a smile.

Everyone in the audience had a shock when they saw Robin's men bring **Pat** on to the stage. Pat had no idea where he was!

And Pat had an even **bigger** shock when his blindfold was taken off. "What on earth am I doing here?" he asked, blushing.

The manager appeared again and handed Pat a big gold cup. "Pat Clifton," he said, "you have been voted Postman of the Year!"

It had been a trick to give Pat the lovely prize! Pat didn't mind at all. He almost cried with happiness as everyone clapped hard!

Pat's puzzle pages

Here are some puzzles I made up for my son Julian.
See if you can get them right!

The answers are on page 61.

Mixed-up names!

Oh dear, the typist got into a muddle
sending these letters to people in
Greendale. Can you work out who
they are for?

deT lenG

1

2

CP byleS

3

rsM nogGigs

taKy gattoPe

4

Spot the city!

Try to write the name of each city in the correct place on the map.

Bristol
Dublin
Glasgow
Llandudno
London
Manchester
Penzance

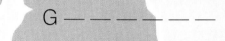

G — — — — — — — —

D — — — — — — —   M — — — — — — — —

L — — — — — — — —

B — — — — — — —

L — — — — — —

P — — — — — — —

Mrs Goggins' broken till

Mrs Goggins' till isn't working properly. Help her to add up the bill correctly!

stamps	60 p
envelopes	40 p
pencil	15 p
wrapping paper	10 p
total	

Engine trouble

Pat felt happy as he started work one snowy morning. "I wonder if I can help anyone today?" he said to Jess with a grin.

It was going to be a busy day, so he stopped to fill up his van with petrol. "Stay inside, Jess. I won't be long," he smiled.

Suddenly an angry dog jumped up and barked at the window. Jess's hair stood on end with fright and he raced out of the van!

Pat picked up Jess and held him safely in the air while he shouted at the dog to go away. Jess purred with delight!

Pat placed Jess back on his seat, got back into the van and set off for the post office.

But, on the way, his van made a funny gurgling noise and shuddered to a stop. "Oh dear, it's engine trouble!" said Pat.

Doctor Gilbertson came past. She listened to the engine with her stethoscope. "Mmm, I can't hear anything wrong," she sighed.

"It's not like a bicycle," said Miss Hubbard. Granny Dryden thought the engine must have been cold and offered to knit a cover for it.

PC Selby took off his helmet and looked under the bonnet. He shook his head and declared, "I think I'll just direct the traffic!"

Even Ted Glen, with all his tools, couldn't help. "Everything seems to be in order," he said, scratching his head.

And then, just as Alf Thompson arrived to tow Pat's van with his tractor, Katy Pottage cried, "I'll bet you've run out of petrol, Pat!"

My helmet!

"Oh no! I forgot to put petrol in when the garage dog jumped up at Jess. Everyone has helped **me** today!" he laughed.

Power-cut in Greendale

Postman Pat stood in front of the mirror and combed his hair. He was very smart in his best suit and bow-tie.

"I must look my best for the village concert," he said to Jess, who wondered why Pat was wearing such strange clothes!

Suddenly all the lights went out and the room was plunged into total darkness.

"Oh dear," murmured Pat. "The storm must have caused a power-cut."

He carried Jess to the kitchen, placed him in his warm basket and then felt his way to the door.

"'Bye, Jess. See you later," he said, as he left the house.

It was a horrid evening. The wind blew hard and the rain poured down. Pat could hardly see through the windows of his van as he drove carefully towards the village.

On the way he saw Miss Hubbard pushing her bicycle along the lane. Her front light had broken and she couldn't see where she was going.

Pat stopped and took her the torch he always carried in his van. He tied it securely to the handlebars of her bicycle and switched it on.

"That's wonderful! Thank you, Pat," smiled Miss Hubbard. "See you at the concert."

As he reached the edge of Greendale, Pat noticed that not a single light was on. He hoped that it wouldn't spoil the concert!

I'd better see if Granny Dryden is all right, he thought, so he stopped again and knocked on her door.

"I'm all dressed up but my hair is still wet," complained Granny Dryden sadly. "My hairdryer won't work without electricity!"

"Come with me then," said Pat. "My van has a lovely warm heater inside. Your hair will soon be dry!"

Walking to the gate, Granny Dryden saw the van's headlights gleaming brightly.

"That's odd," she said. "If there's a power-cut, why are **your** lights on?"

Pat smiled at Granny's silly mistake. Didn't she understand that cars and vans run off batteries?

At the Church Hall they met Reverend Timms, who was pacing around with a worried look on his face.

"Ah, nice to see you, Pat. Hello, Granny Dryden." He sighed deeply. "If only the electricity would come back on. I don't want to cancel the concert."

Just at that moment the lights did come on! Now Pat could see all the other performers who were going to sing or play musical instruments. There was Ted Glen . . . and Peter Fogg . . . and over there, Colonel Forbes!

"Hello, Dad!" cried Julian, greeting his father with a big hug. He was holding his recorder, and Pat was very proud of him.

At last it was seven o'clock and the concert was about to begin! Everyone was silent as Reverend Timms explained that it was in aid of raising money to mend the church roof. But then something dreadful happened! There was a loud clap of thunder, a dazzling fork of lightning and all the lights went out **again**! Everyone groaned.

"What shall we do?" wailed Reverend Timms' voice from the darkness.

"Don't worry," came Pat's voice. "I can help!"

He **did** help, too! Within a few minutes the concert carried on because Pat drove his van up to the doors of the Hall and switched on his headlights!

The evening was a great success, thanks to Pat. Everyone sang in tune, and Julian played his recorder beautifully. In fact, people said afterwards that the concert seemed especially enjoyable, held in the twinkling light from Pat's van!

Seeing double!

These pictures may look the same but there are 12 little differences. See if you can spot them all, then turn to page 61 and find out if you're right!

Just Jess!

Pet Show problems

It was the day of the Greendale Pet Show and all the animals were getting ready to be judged. Can you guess who was one of the judges?

Yes, it was Pat! Now, because Pat was a judge, Jess couldn't enter the contest, but that didn't stop him from entering the Church Hall!

Grrrrr!

There was trouble brewing down below! Jess spotted a dog he had seen before – a dog that had **chased** him before!

Now the dog was chasing Jess again! "Stop!" cried Pat in alarm. But the poor cat was too scared to even **think** of stopping!

25

The rest of the animals joined in the fun and soon the Pet Show was in a dreadful muddle. If **only** Pat could catch Jess . . .

Pat dived to the floor and managed to grab hold of Jess. "Got you!" he panted, putting him safely inside his jacket.

Pat and Julia took Jess outside to the van. "Poor Jess," said Pat, stroking him gently. "You shouldn't have followed me!"

It was judging time and **what** a job it was! In the end, Pat, Miss Hubbard and PC Selby gave prizes to **all** the pets!

Pottage Cottage

It was a sunny spring morning, the first day of April, when Postman Pat stopped his van in the yard of Greendale Farm and let out Julian and his friend Bill.

"Have a good time with Tom and Katy!" shouted Pat with a wave. Then he drove away.

The boys walked up to the farmhouse, but before they could knock, Julian saw a note pinned to the big front door. It read:

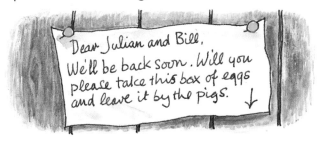

Dear Julian and Bill,
We'll be back soon. Will you please take this box of eggs and leave it by the pigs. ↓

The arrow pointed to a large cardboard box on the step. Julian and Bill were pleased to help, so they each took an end of the box and struggled back across the yard with it.

"Phew – this is heavy!" gasped Bill. "It feels as if it's full of **rocks**!"

After stopping twice to rest, they reached the gate and placed the box carefully near the gate post.

"Hope we haven't broken any of the eggs!" said Julian, wiping his brow. "I'd better take a look."

When he opened the box he had a surprise. "Hey, this box **is** full of rocks!"

"And here's another note!" cried Bill, seeing a piece of paper lying on the seat of an old milking stool.

Sorry to bother you, boys, but will you please leave this milking stool by the big field for Daisy the cow!

The boys were puzzled to find this second note, but they picked up the stool and tramped off to the big field.

When they arrived they put the stool near the fence.

"This is a waste of time," panted Bill. "That's not a cow in the field – it's a **bull**! It has a ring through its nose!"

"There's something funny going on here!" said Julian, picking up yet **another** note, which was tied to a ladder.

Just one more job, boys! Please carry this ladder to Pottage Cottage. It is needed to mend the thatched roof.

"Pottage Cottage? Never heard of it!" mumbled Julian.

"It must be round here somewhere," said Bill. "Let's walk round the farm and find it."

Holding the long ladder, they wandered around the fields but there was no sign of a cottage. Soon they met Peter Fogg, driving his big tractor, and they asked him.

"Pottage Cottage?" he smiled. "Yes, it's at the side of the farmhouse!"

Back they went to the farmhouse and walked round and round it.

"There it is!" cried Bill at last, pointing to a dog kennel with a neat little thatched roof.

"Bah, another joke!" said Julian. "No one needs a ladder to reach that roof!"

Then they heard giggles coming from the kennel and it started to rock from side to side! The boys rushed over to it. Tom and Katy Pottage scrambled out, almost falling over with laughter.

"**April fools**!" shouted the twins.

"Oh dear, we really have been a pair of fools!" agreed Julian and Bill, starting to laugh too!

But they didn't mind at all, because the twins took them back to the farmhouse for orange juice and biscuits. Then they spent the rest of the day playing and having lots of fun!

Through the maize!

Peter Fogg has a surprise for the Pottage twins. With his tractor he has made a maze in the maize field! Can you lead Katy and Tom to the bottle of lemonade he has left for them in the middle of the field?

Where's Jess?
A mystery story

'Bye, Mrs Goggins!

Look at these pictures of Pat when he was delivering the post one morning. At the end you'll find there is a mystery to solve!

One morning Pat left the post office to take the day's letters to the folk of Greendale.

Good morning, Pat!

PAT 1

He called at Granny Dryden's . . .

. . . and then at Miss Hubbard's.

After he gave a parcel to Reverend Timms . . .

Then he went up to Thompson Ground. There he had a cup of tea with Dorothy.

At Ted Glen's workshop, he picked up Julian's bicycle wheel, which Ted had mended.

Jess! Where are you?

Back at Mrs Goggins' . . . and Jess is **missing**!

Well, do **you** know where Jess is? Look for a clue!

The answer is on page 61.

Draw-it-yourself

How would you like to have Pat, his van and Jess on your bedroom wall? With a pencil and paper, trace or copy the outlines below, then colour them using crayons or felt-tip pens. Do lots and ask a grown-up to stick them in a line on your wall.

Seaside holiday

Pat lay back on the golden sand and closed his eyes. He loved the warm sun and the cool wind that blew from the sea.

"This is the life," he said. "No more letters to post for two weeks!"

But then he shivered as he felt icy hands grab his arm. It was Julian, dripping wet from splashing about in the water.

"Time for tea, Dad!" cried Julian.

"Yes, it is," agreed Sara. "Let's go back to the hotel."

Pat, Sara, Julian and his friend Bill went to their room to change out of their swimming costumes. They were staying on holiday at Seaview, a big hotel on the promenade.

Pat sat down at the dressing-table and looked at a handful of brightly coloured post cards. He picked up a pen but he didn't **write** anything. Instead, he scratched his head, shook the pen a few times and then put it down again with a sigh.

"Ready?" asked Julian.

Pat nodded and then went downstairs with the others to the dining-room.

That afternoon, they went to the pleasure beach, where they had lots of fun on the rides. Julian liked the Ghost Train. Bill loved the Waltzer, though he looked quite green after **three** rides!

Next, the boys went into the sand-pit, where grown-ups were not allowed. So Pat sat with Sara at a nearby table and licked an ice-cream.

"I brought these for you to write out and send to people back in Greendale," said Sara, opening her handbag and placing Pat's post cards in front of him.

"I haven't got my pen," replied Pat.

"Here's one!"

"Ah, thank you." Pat didn't look very pleased.

"Oh, Pat!" laughed Sara. "Will you **ever** send them? Poor Mrs Goggins, Granny Dryden and everyone else will be missing you!"

"Sorry," said Pat, blushing. "I keep **starting** to write but I just can't seem to do it."

"It's too much like work!" smiled Sara.

Pat grinned at her and started to write, but Julian and Bill ran up and asked to go to the swimming pool.

"All right," said Pat, putting the post cards into his pocket. "I'll do these later."

Next morning Pat still hadn't written his cards. When he came downstairs with Sara, Julian and Bill, he found the manager in a terrible muddle. The letter rack had fallen off the wall in the hall and the guests' letters were lying all over the desk and floor.

"What a mess!" cried the manager. "Everyone will be asking for their letters but I haven't time to sort them out, as I must help in the kitchen!"

"Don't worry!" said Pat. "I'm just the person you need!"

He hooked the rack on the wall, then, with Julian's and Bill's help, he picked up all the scattered letters and began to put them back in their right places.

"I can see you know exactly what you're doing!" beamed the manager. And off he went to cook breakfast.

"I **enjoyed** helping," said Pat when he'd finished.

"You deserve your breakfast after all that hard work," said Sara.

"Yes, but first I have another job to do," laughed Pat, taking his post cards from his pocket and starting to write. "After doing that, I'm just in the mood for sending out my **cards**!"

Counting sheep

Pat was tired after working hard all morning but he stopped to stroke Lizzie at Thompson Ground. "Where's Alf today?" he asked.

"He's trying to count the sheep," Dorothy told him. "He needs me, but I'm waiting for the blacksmith." "I'll help him!" said Pat.

Alf was finding his job very hard. "There are so many sheep, I keep losing count," he explained. "Show me what to do," said Pat.

Alf told Pat to sit by the fence and count the sheep as they jumped into the pen. "This is **easy** work!" smiled Pat.

But it wasn't easy because there's no better way of getting to sleep than counting sheep! Pat started to **yawn**.

Soon all the sheep were in their pen. "How many are there?" asked Alf. Pat didn't answer because he was **fast asleep**!

When he woke up, Pat thought of a clever way to keep track of the sheep. He put an air-mail sticker on each one he counted!

Taking the stickers off again was tiring too. "Coming for a coffee?" asked Alf. "No thanks," said Pat. "I'm going for a **rest**!"

Colouring time

PC Selby's daughter Lucy has drawn this lovely picture of Greendale but she needs help with colouring it in. Can you finish it for her?

A race around Greendale

It's the day of the Greendale Summer Fair and you and your friends can join in the fun of the village race! It's easy to play. Start at Mrs Goggins' post office and throw the die to move your counter. The winner is the first person to reach Greendale Farm, where there are sandwiches, drinks and a bouncy castle waiting!

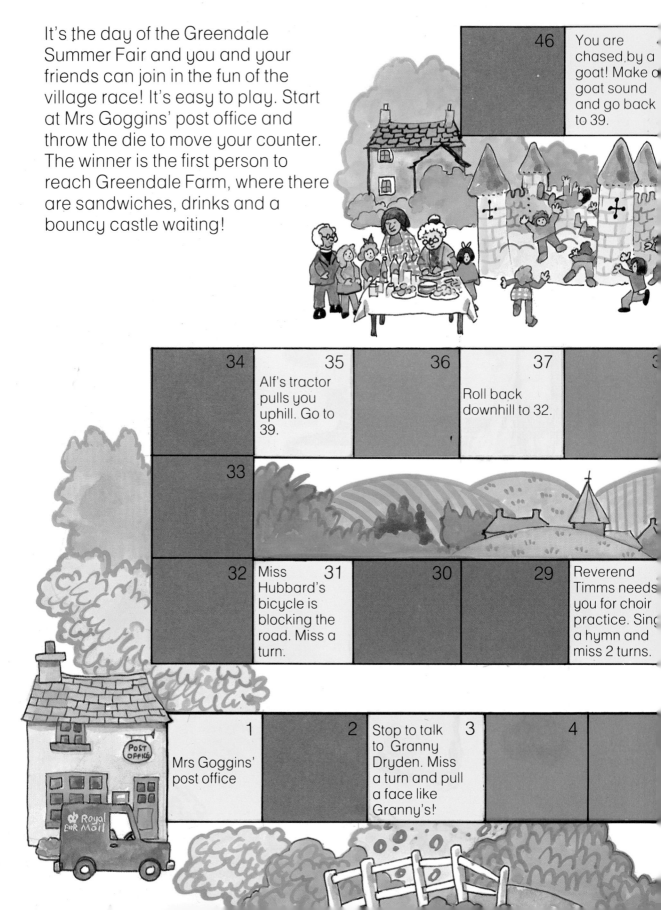

46

You are chased by a goat! Make a goat sound and go back to 39.

34

35 Alf's tractor pulls you uphill. Go to 39.

36

37 Roll back downhill to 32.

33

32

31 Miss Hubbard's bicycle is blocking the road. Miss a turn.

30

29 Reverend Timms needs you for choir practice. Sing a hymn and miss 2 turns.

1 Mrs Goggins' post office

2

3 Stop to talk to Granny Dryden. Miss a turn and pull a face like Granny's!

4

44

43 Cow in the road! Miss a turn and make a mooing noise!

42

41 Colonel Forbes shows you the way. Go to 44.

39

40

19

18

17

20

16

21

15 Ted Glen tunes up your car. Make a noise like an engine and go to 21.

22

14

23 PC Selby is directing the traffic. Miss a turn.

13

27

26

25

24

Buy a drink from Sam's mobile shop. Miss 2 turns and make a slurping noise! **12**

6

7 Take a short cut along the lane.

8

9

10

11

Ship ahoy!

"Here's a parcel marked **URGENT** for Peter Fogg," said Pat, sorting his post one Saturday morning. "I'd better take it to him quickly!"

"This is for Peter," said Pat to Julia Pottage. "Oh, you've just missed him!" she replied. "He's gone boating for the day."

Peter was having a great time in his little boat. "A life on the ocean wave . . ." he sang as he whizzed about.

But after enjoying a picnic lunch afloat, he found that the engine wouldn't start! "Oh, no!" he cried. "I'm **stuck**!"

"Ahoy there, Peter!" came a voice he knew from a small rowing boat. Was it **really** Postman Pat and Julian coming to the rescue?

"Julian and I decided to have some fun this afternoon **and** bring you this important package at the same time!" Pat explained.

Peter was delighted. "It's the new part I ordered for my boat's engine. Now we'll soon have her going again!"

Back to shore the **easy** way! Peter rewarded his rescuers by giving them a tow back. Julian was pleased. He was tired of rowing!

Your own post office

How would you like to have your own post office? With a little help from a grown-up, you can make a counter with a big piece of cardboard or box lid. Then copy out and colour in money, stamps, postal orders and TV licences, as shown below. An empty wooden salt-shaker makes a good pretend rubber stamp. Add a few envelopes and you'll have a post office that even Mrs Goggins would be proud of!

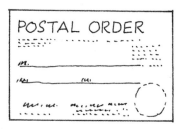

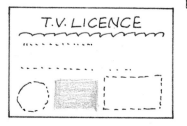

Miss Hubbard's indoor garden

Would you like to make a beautiful little garden for your window sill? Lay a sheet of blotting paper in a shallow tray and place a carrot-top (**ask a parent to cut it for you**) in the centre. Add a pathway of tiny stones and then scatter mustard or cress seeds over the rest of your garden. Stand it on a sunny window sill, keep the blotting paper damp by watering it carefully every day, and soon you should have a lovely lawn complete with a carrot bush!

If you enjoy watching things grow, perhaps you could start a mini-garden outside with flowers or bulbs!

Parcel post

At the post office there was a giant parcel for Doctor Gilbertson, but it was too big to fit in Pat's van!

"It's no use," sighed Pat. But then PC Selby came past and helped him to push the parcel on to the roof of the van.

"It looks as if it's going to rain," said Pat on the way to Doctor Gilbertson's. "You won't like that, will you, Jess?"

Oh, no! Doctor Gilbertson was out visiting her patients, and now her parcel was beginning to get very wet indeed!

I mustn't let the rain damage it, thought Pat. There was only one thing to do — take it back to the post office!

"Look after it for me, Mrs Goggins," panted Pat. "I must go and do my other deliveries now. I'm late with them."

Later, Pat returned to Doctor Gilbertson's. But why did she start laughing when he told her how he'd tried to keep the parcel dry?

"It's my new garden pond!" explained Doctor Gilbertson. "So it's going to spend its whole life wet!" Poor Pat felt very silly!

The flying postman!

The little red post office van wove its way along the leafy country lanes to Greendale Farm. Jess sat by Pat's side, keeping a watchful eye on the birds hopping off the hedges and soaring into the sky. How he wished **he** could fly!

At the farm, Pat and Jess were amazed to find a small yellow helicopter. Two men stood by it, and with them were Julia Pottage and Baby Paul.

"Here's Pat now!" cried Julia, as Pat walked up to her. "He'll help you!"

"Hello," said one of the men, who was holding a big camera. "I'm a film director and I've come to film Greendale. Mrs Pottage says you could show me where all the prettiest places are!"

"I'd love to," replied Pat sadly, "but I'm so busy with the post, I haven't time."

"What a pity," said the director. "Mrs Pottage says you know Greendale better than anyone else."

Pat handed Julia her letters and then returned to his van. Jess spotted a blackbird picking up a small crust of bread, and he chased it playfully. The bird was scared and it dropped its food as it flew away.

"That's naughty, Jess!" cried Pat, picking up the bread and throwing it back to the bird.

Then he stroked his chin thoughtfully. "Hmm, seeing that little bird drop its bread has given me an idea!" he said.

Soon the people of Greendale were in for a shock! Alf and Dorothy Thompson gazed in wonder as the yellow helicopter appeared out of the skies and landed by their gate.

Colonel Forbes spilled cornflakes down his shirt when the helicopter stopped on his front lawn. Sam almost crashed when it zoomed low over his mobile shop. And Reverend Timms thought he was seeing things when he felt a strong gust of wind from behind and turned to find a flying machine in his grounds!

Pat was delivering the post by helicopter and showing the film director all the sights! He loved every minute of it as he sat, with Jess on his knee, between the pilot and the director, who was filming.

There was nowhere to land in the village itself, but Pat had **more** clever ideas! Miss Hubbard was wheeling her bicycle through her gate when her post came down from the sky on a rope and landed on her handlebars! And Granny Dryden's letters landed neatly in front of her as she did her gardening!

A few weeks later the film director sent a copy of his film to Pat, and Reverend Timms showed it on a big screen in the Church Hall. Everyone was thrilled to see the beautiful views of Greendale from the air and they all clapped loudly when they read a message at the end which said **Special thanks to Pat Clifton**.

"May I have your autograph?" Lucy Selby asked Pat shyly, and everyone laughed.

Only **one** person wasn't keen to see the film, and that was Jess. You see, it reminded him of that nasty ride in the sky! He wasn't jealous of the birds any more. From now on he was going to keep all four paws firmly on the ground!

Pat's puzzles

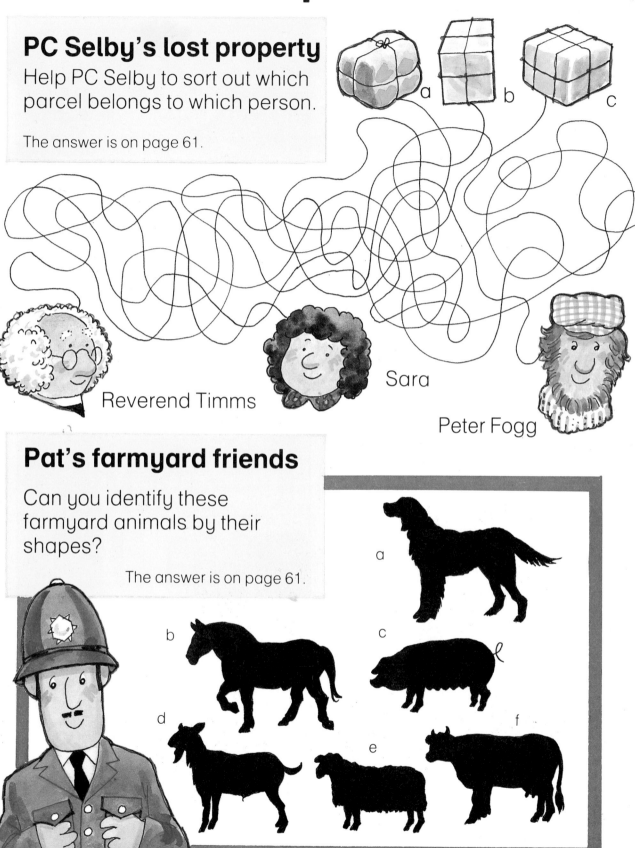

PC Selby's lost property

Help PC Selby to sort out which parcel belongs to which person.

The answer is on page 61.

a

b

c

Reverend Timms

Sara

Peter Fogg

Pat's farmyard friends

Can you identify these farmyard animals by their shapes?

The answer is on page 61.

a

b

c

d

e

f

Mrs Goggins to the rescue!

In the post office, Katy Pottage saw some crayons for sale. "Look, Mum!" she said, putting her baby doll on the counter.

Whoops! Baby Laura fell down and landed in Pat's postbag. But she didn't hurt herself, as letters are quite soft!

It was time to go but there was no sign of Laura. "I left her here!" cried Katy. Pat had no idea he had a passenger in his bag!

After a careful search, Mrs Goggins said, "She must be in Pat's bag!" But it was too late. Pat was off to Pencaster!

"I **must** catch him!" puffed Mrs Goggins, borrowing Miss Hubbard's bicycle. "Laura will get lost in Pencaster post office!"

Riding a bicycle was hard work for Mrs Goggins, so she was pleased when Sam gave her a lift in his mobile shop!

Sam had to stop to serve his customers but luckily Doctor Gilbertson was passing. "Jump in and come with **me**!" she smiled.

Soon they reached the town of Pencaster. "Hurray, I can see Pat's van ahead!" shouted Doctor Gilbertson in excitement.

But she was wrong! Pat and Jess were having a drink in a café and were amazed to see Mrs Goggins and the Doctor race past!

At Pencaster post office the red van stopped. "Pat! Pat!" cried Mrs Goggins, but then she found she had made a mistake!

"Oh, we've lost Pat **and** Baby Laura!" sighed Mrs Goggins. Then she heard Pat's voice say, "Are you looking for **this**?"

When Pat saw Mrs Goggins pass the café, he guessed something was wrong and looked in his bag! Katy soon had her baby back!

55

The Colonel's party

Sara came downstairs in a beautiful pink evening gown and went into the front room.

"How do I look, Pat?" she asked her husband, turning round slowly like a model.

"Wow!" said Pat. "You look like a **queen**!"

"You look like a **king**!" laughed Sara, buttoning the jacket of Pat's smart suit and straightening his glasses.

"And here's Prince Julian!" added Pat, as their son joined them in his best clothes and with his hair neatly brushed.

Jess wove in and out of their legs. He knew they were going out somewhere special and he wanted to be with them.

"Sorry, we can't take you." Pat picked him up and stroked him behind the ears. "Cats aren't invited to Colonel Forbes' Harvest-time Party!"

Driving through the rain, they reached the village and took the lonely road that led towards Colonel Forbes' big mansion. But suddenly the van felt very bumpy and kept pulling to one side.

"Oh dear, it's a puncture," tutted Pat. "Everyone **out**!"

Sara and Julian waited patiently while Pat changed the wheel. It didn't take long, but when he'd finished he was very messy. His hands were dirty and he had smudges of dirt on his cheeks and forehead. Worse still, he had big wet patches on his knees from kneeling on the muddy ground.

Soon they were on their way again, but it wasn't long before they came across a car they all knew. It was Reverend Timms' old Morris Minor, and its back wheels were stuck in the mud.

"A little push should do the trick!" said Reverend Timms.

Pat, Julian and Sara went round to the back of his car and pushed hard while Reverend Timms revved up the engine. Suddenly the car lurched forward and gripped the road again, but not before the wheels had spun round and sprayed Sara and Julian from head to toe with mud!

Reverend Timms didn't notice. He simply waved, shouted, "Thank you!" and carried on.

"I wonder why he's dressed like a pixie?" said Julian.

Pat rang the bell at Colonel Forbes' house. He was going to tell him what had happened and then he, Sara and Julian would return home to change. But when the door opened, they were amazed to see that everyone was wearing a funny costume. There was a knight, a sailor, a Roman soldier, Robin Hood, a giant cat like Jess, and Reverend Timms in his pixie suit!

"Oh," groaned Pat. "I **forgot** it was a fancy-dress party!"

"Ah, come in, come in!" beamed Colonel Forbes. "I see you've all come as tramps. Very good costumes, I must say!"

So Pat, Sara and Julian enjoyed their night at the party after all! They had a great time dancing to the music played by the band, and they enjoyed a tasty supper too. But, best of all, when the time came to judge the best fancy-dress costumes, they won first prize!

"It was worth getting dirty for, wasn't it?" said Pat, wiping specks of mud from his glasses.

Julian nodded, but Sara didn't answer. She would have preferred to keep her pretty dress clean!

The Greendale ghost

It was a dark, misty evening in autumn and Alf was driving his tractor slowly home along the lane to Thompson Ground.

His lights picked out a spooky white shape drifting through the mist lying over the road ahead! Then it disappeared quickly!

Next day Miss Hubbard went for a ride on her bicycle. It was quite late when she returned and very dark too!

"Aaargh! A g-ghost!" she cried, seeing the strange flapping white thing in front of her. She rode straight into a ditch!

Soon everyone was talking about the ghost. Dorothy Thompson said something was even taking the washing off her clothes-line!

Early the following morning, it was Pat's and Jess's turn to see the ghost. Jess's eyes almost popped out of his head!

Pat stopped his van and jumped out. He didn't really believe in ghosts but he shivered when it slowly came towards him!

"Woof!" said the ghost. It was a dog all tangled in a sheet! "No wonder Dorothy's washing keeps going missing!" laughed Pat.

Answers

Mixed-up names! (page 14): 1 Ted Glen; 2 PC Selby; 3 Mrs Goggins; 4 Katy Pottage.

Spot the city! (page 15)

Mrs Goggins' broken till (page 15): The total is £1.25.

Seeing double! (page 22):

Where's Jess? (page 30): Look carefully at the picture of Dorothy Thompson's kitchen and you'll see Jess getting into the basket. And that's exactly where Pat found him – fast asleep!

PC Selby's lost property (page 51): a Sara; b Reverend Timms; c Peter Fogg.

Pat's farmyard friends (page 51): a dog; b horse; c pig; d goat; e sheep; f cow.

Cheerio!

I hope you enjoyed all the stories about Greendale. It's a lovely place to be a postman, isn't it?

It's time for us to go now, but Jess and I are looking forward to being with you again soon. And we'll have lots more of our adventures to tell you about!

Oh, yes, one more thing . . . I've written down the words to our song. So next time you see us on TV, don't forget to sing along!

'Bye for now. Love from *Pat*